Joseph Skipsey

A Book of Lyrics, Including Songs, Ballads, and Chants

Joseph Skipsey

A Book of Lyrics, Including Songs, Ballads, and Chants

ISBN/EAN: 9783744787109

Printed in Europe, USA, Canada, Australia, Japan

Cover: Foto ©Andreas Hilbeck / pixelio.de

More available books at **www.hansebooks.com**

A

Book of Lyrics,

INCLUDING

Songs, Ballads,

AND

Chants.

A

Book of Lyrics,

INCLUDING

Songs, Ballads,

AND

Chants.

BY

JOSEPH SKIPSEY.

morth Nicol?

NEW EDITION, REVISED.

LONDON:

DAVID BOGUE, 3, ST. MARTIN'S PLACE.

1881.

Printed by
Blades, East & Blades,
Abchurch Lane, London.

17

CONTENTS.

PREFACE.

PARTLY from deference to the opinion of a few well-wishers, and partly from an impression that it would be proper so to do, I beg leave to state that the author of the following Lyrics is a coal-miner, and that he was sent into the coal-pits of Percy Main, near North Shields, to help to earn his bread while yet a mere child, and when the sum total of his learning consisted in his ability to read his A.B.C., or at most his A.B. ab card. When it is stated that the requirements of the times at that period necessitated the young to be in the mines from twelve to fourteen hours per day, it will be seen that they had little leisure for self-culture, and that only by dint of perseverance, and by not allowing the few spare moments to remain un-utilized that should present themselves, could those who had a desire, acquire anything in the shape of education. The author being

B

possessed with the requisite aspiration, soon had .felt
what is thus expressed, and instead of spending his
hours on the play-ground, he devoted his Sundays and
other holidays to the acquisition of the ability to read,
and to decipher simple arithmetical questions. These
operations were usually performed in his mother's
garret (he had no father—the father having lost his
life when the writer was a baby " in arms "), whilst he
learned himself to write with a piece of chalk on his
trap-door—a door connected with the ventilation of
the mine, and which it was his duty to attend. In
this rude way were his studies pursued, and with what
success may be indicated by the fact that, before he
was eleven years old, he had formed the romantic
notion of trying to commit the Bible to memory, and
that he had actually acquired a number of the chapters
by " heart," and was only prevented from proceeding
further by the ridicule of a grey-bearded wiseacre, to
whom he had the temerity to disclose his project. By
the time he was sixteen years old he had, from a
Lindley Murray, which had been presented to him by
an aunt, and through much effort and perseverance,
acquired a knowledge of the elements of English
Grammar. Other studies, chiefly of a scientific nature,
succeeded this ; then that of poetry, or rather the
poetry of celebrated poets, as Shakespeare, Milton,

and Burns, for otherwise the love of the muses had grown up with him from his infancy, and he had actually practised verse-making, while he was yet a child behind his trap-door. '

After the elapse of a few more years, and after making repeated efforts, and in vain, to get a suitable situation out of the mine, he printed a batch of lyrics (1859), which earned him the respect of several eminent persons in the North of England. Through the kindness of one of these he was placed into the office of sub-store-keeper at the Gateshead Iron Works This was at the commencement of the year 1859, and at the latter part of the year 1863 he was placed, on the commendation of the same kind friend, as sub-librarian to the Literary and Philosophical Society, Newcastle-upon-Tyne. This latter office, which was certainly extremely congenial to his tastes, he only held a few months, when, from the inadequacy of the income to meet his domestic needs, he was necessitated to give it up, again to find himself a toiler in the coal mines. In 1871 he again resorted to the printer, and issued a small volume of poems, which obtained a kindly notice not only from the *Newcastle Chronicle* and the rest of the local papers, but also from many of the London weeklies, including the *Literary World* and the *Sunday Times*, and also a kind word from the

Athenæum and the *Spectator ;* whilst several of the pieces included in this issue were honored by a translation into the French tongue, and published in the *Beautés de la Poesie de Anglaise par le Chevalier De Chatelain.* The encouragement thus received has helped to stimulate the author to persevere in his attempts at self-culture, and the embodiment, when the impulse has come upon him, of his sentiments and feelings in verse, until he finds himself in possession of material for the present book—a book which he now submits to the public in the hope that it may at once prove of some interest to the peruser, and be the means of rendering some little personal benefit to himself.

In conclusion, the author would say, that should the present venture, several of the pieces of which have already seen the light, find favour with the public, it may in due time be succeeded by a companion volume—a book of Songs and Ditties,* and in the two brochures thus offered, would be comprised nearly the whole of his verse that the author would care to put into print.

JOSEPH SKIPSEY.

---

* As in this re-issue, a selection from these effusions has been inserted to supply the places of several pieces on speculative subjects, which the author has deemed it advisable to omit, the work Songs and Ditties is not now contemplated.—J. S.

A BOOK OF LYRICS.

LO, A FAIRY.

Lo, a fairy on a day
Came and bore my heart away ;
But as she secured her prize,
Sweetest smiles illumed her eyes,
   And, hey, lerry O !

From that moment my career
Lay thro' dells and dingles, where
Pleasure blossom'd out of pain—
Where grief changed her dying strain
   To "hey, lerry O !"

MY MERRY BIRD.

I HAD a merry bird
   Who sung a merry song,
And take it on my word,
   The day it was not long
In the presence of my bird with its merry, merry song.

Did fortune strew my way
  With crosses, which, to bear
Had rendered me a prey
  To sorrow or despair—
My birdie trilled its lay, and they vanished into air.

And thus went things with me,
  Till lo, with sudden sweep,
Death came across the lea
  And laid my bird asleep;   [weep.
And ever since that hour I've done nought but sigh and

ANNIE.

COAL black are the tresses of Fanny,
  But never a mortal could see
The coal-colour'd tresses of Annie,
  And be as a body should be.

White, white, is her forehead, and bonnie—
  And, when she goes down to the well,
The beat of the footstep of Annie,
  The wrath of a tiger would quell.

Red, red are her round cheeks and bonnie—
  And when she is knitting, her tone—
The charm of the accents of Annie,
  Would ravish the heart of a stone.

Nay, rare are her graces and many,
  But nothing whatever can be
Compared to the sweet glance of Annie,—
  The glance she has given to me.

AWAY TO THE WELL.

Away to the well lilted Annie—
  Away with her skiel to the well ;
Away to the well whistled Johnnie,
  The pride and delight of the dell.

Sweet, sweet is the well ; but, ah, sweeter,
  The words of the silver-tongued elf ;
And I counsel the youth who shall meet her,
  To keep a strict guard on himself.

Deep, deep is the well ; but, ah, deeper,
  The guile of the silver-tongued elf ;
And the laugher she'll turn to a weeper,
  Unless he look well to himself.

'Twas thus proved the mortal to Johnnie :
  Lo, pale, now, he wanders the dell,—
Pale, pale with the potion that Annie
  Had caused him to drink at the well.

BEREAVED.

One day as I came down by Jarrow,
  Engirt by a crowd on a stone,
A woman sat moaning and sorrow
  Seized all who gave heed to her moan.

" Nay, blame not my sad lamentation,
  But oh, let " she said, " my tears flow,
Nay offer me no consolation—-
  I know they are dead down below.

" I heard the dread blast and I darted
    Away on the road to the pit,
Nor stopped till my senses departed,
    And left me the wretch I here sit.

" Ah, thus let me sit, " so entreated
    She those who had had her away ;
Then yet on the hard granite seated,
    Resumed her lament and did say :—

" My mother, poor body, would harry
    Me oft with a look sad and pale,
When I had determined to marry
    The dimpled-chinn'd lad of the dale.

" Not that she had any objection
    To one praised by each and by all ;
But ay his lot caused a reflection
    That still, still her bosom would gall.

" Nay, blame not my sad lamentation ;
    My mother sleeps under the yew—
She views not the dire desolation
    She dreaded one day I should view.

" Bedabbled with blood are my tresses?
    No matter ! Unlock not my hand !—
When first I enjoyed his caresses,
    Their hue would his praises command.

" He'll never praise more locks nor features,
    Nor, when the long day-tide is o'er,
With me view our two happy creatures,
    With bat and with ball at the door.

"Nay, chide not. A pair either bolder
  Or better nobody could see :
They passed for a year or two older
  Than what I could prove them to be.

" Their equals for courage and action
  Were not to be found in the place ;
And others might boast of attraction,
  But none had their colour or grace.

" Their feelings were such, tho' when smitten
  By scorn, still their blood would rebel,
They wept for the little blind kitten
  Our neighbour did drown in the well.

" The same peaceful, calm, and brave bearing,
  Had still been the father's was theirs ;
And now we felt older a-wearing,
  We deemed they'd soon lighten our cares.

" So deemed I last night   On his shoulder
  I hung and beheld them at play :
I dreamed not how soon they must moulder
  Down, down in their cold bed of clay.

" Chide, chide not.   This sad lamentation
  But endeth the burden began,
When to the whole dale's consternation,
  Our second was crushed by the van.

" That dark day the words of my mother
  In all the deep tone which had made
Me like a wind-ridden leaf dother,
  Rang like the dead bell in my head.

" Despair, the grim bird away chidden,
  Would light on the house-top again ;
But still from my husband was hidden
  Each thought that had put him to pain

" He's pass'd from existence unharried
  By any forbodings of mine ;
Nor till we the lisper had buried,
  E'er pined he.   But then he did pine

" Adown when the shadow had falling
  Across the long row gable-end,
He miss'd him as home from his calling,
  With thrice weary bones he would wend.

" No more would his heavy step lighten,
  No more would his hazel eyes glow,
No more would his smutty face brighten
  At sight of the darling.   Ah, no !

" He lived by my bodings unharried,
  But when from his vision and mine,
Away the sweet lisper was carried,
  He pined, and long after would pine.

" Ay, truly.—And reason.—The sonsy—
  The bairn with his hair bright and curled,
He still had appeared to our fancy,
  The bonniest bairn in the world.

" As ruddy was he as a cherry,
  With dimple on chin and on cheek ;
And never another as merry
  Was seen to play hide-and-go-seek.

" He, yet with his fun and affection,
  His canny bit pranks and his grace,
He wheedled my heart from dejection,
  And put a bright look on my face.

" Full oft upon one leg advancing,
  Across to the door he would go,
Wheel round on his heel, then go dancing
  With hop after hop down the row.

" When—Let my hand go !—When he perish'd,
  The rest were a balm to my woe :
But now, what remains to be cherish'd ?
  But now, what remains to me now ?

" Barely cold was the pet ere affected
  By fever they lay one and all ;
But lay not like others neglected ;
  I slept not to be at their call.

" Day and night, night and day without slumber,
  I watched till a-weary and worn ;—
When Death took the gem of the number,
  I'd barely strength left me to mourn.

" I've mourn'd enough since.   And tho' cruel
  Mishap like a curs'd hag would find
Her way to my door still, the jewel
  Has seldom been out of my mind.

" Another so light and so airy
  Ne'er gladden'd a fond mother's sight—
I oft heard her called a wee fairy,
  And heard her so called with delight.

" Whilst others played, by me she tarried,
   —The cherub !—and rumour avers
That now-a-days many are married,
   With not half the sense that was hers.

" A-down on the hearth-rug a-sitting
   The long winter nights she was heard,
The while her sweet fingers were knitting,
   To lilt out her lay like a bird.

" Did I appear cross ?   To me stealing,
   Askance in my face she would keek,
At which, e'er the victim of feeling,
   I could not but pat her bit cheek.

" She once, when I'd pricked this hard finger—
   No he who in grave-clothes first slept ;
No she—with the senses that linger
   I cannot tell which of them—wept.

" She vanished at last.   Ah, an ocean
   Of trouble appeared that black cup ;
But what was it all to the potion
   I now am commanded to sup ?

" My husband, my birdies, my blossoms !
   Well—well—I am wicked—yes, yes ;
But take my case home to your bosoms,
   And say if your sins would be less ?

" The dear ones to perish thus sudden—
   Not only last night by the hearth—
This morn when resuming their dudden,
   E'en they, the dear bairns, were all mirth.

" Aroused by their voices—a-yearning
   To kiss them I sprang to the floor,
They kissed me and bade me good morning,
   And whistled away from the door.

" Long after away they had hurried,
   Their music a-rang in my ears ;
Then thought I of those we had buried,
   And thought of the jewels with tears.

" Then thought I—what said I—thus thinking
   Was I, when rat-tat went the pane,
And back into sense again shrinking,
   I into bed stumbled again.

" Did I sleep? I did weep. To his calling
   The father had gone hours before,
And now in that havock appalling,
   He lies with the blossoms I bore.

" Did I sleep? I did weep. Heart-a-weary,
   How oft have I so wept before,
Not to sleep but to weep, lone and dreary
   I've wandered the broken brick floor.

" Did I sleep—well, your kind arm and steady
   My tottering steps, and now you
Go, get out the winding sheets ready,
   And do what remaineth to do.

" Spread winding sheets—one for the father,
   And two for the darlings, our pride,—
And one for the wife and the mother,
   Ah, soundly she'll sleep by their side !"

THE VIOLET AND THE ROSE.

THE Violet invited my kiss,—
    I kiss'd it and called it my bride;
"Was ever one slighted like this?"
    Sighed the Rose as it stood by my side.

My heart ever open to grief,
    To comfort the fair one I turned;
"Of fickle ones thou art the chief!"
    Frowned the Violet, and pouted and mourned

Then to end all disputes, I entwined
    The love-stricken blossoms in one;
But that instant their beauty declined,
    And I wept for the deed I had done!

THE DANCE.

MET we in the festal hall,
    Met—our feelings blended!
Love alone shall lead the ball,
    Truth alone shall end it.

Wakes an air, and here and there,
    Soon the dance we tread, when
Ladies bright admire the knight,
    Gallant knights the maiden.

Here and there, an envied pair
  Mid the bright we shimmer ;
Cheer right rare responds to cheer,
  Brimmer clinks with brimmer.

Dance we still, and dance we till
  On our vision waneth
Every light that gilds the night,
  And love in triumph reigneth.

Praised by all we left the hall,
  But, within us ever,
Rapture's self still lead a ball
  Peace should end—ah ! never.

THE REIGN OF GOLD.

It sounded in castle and palace,
  It sounded in cottage and shed,
It sped over mountains and valleys,
  And withered the earth as it sped ;
Like a blast in its fell consummation
  Of all that we holy should hold,
Thrilled, thrilled thro' the nerves of the nation,
  A cry for the reign of King Gold.

Upstarted the chiefs of the city,
  And sending it back with a ring,
To the air of a popular ditty,
  Erected a throne to the king ;

'Twas based upon fiendish persuasions,
  Cemented by crimes manifold :
Embellished by specious ovations,
  That dazzled the foes of King Gold.

The prey of unruly emotion,
  The miner and diver go forth,
And the depths of the earth and the ocean
  Are shorn of their lustre and worth ;
The mountain is riven asunder,
  The days of the valley are told ;
And sinew, and glory, and grandeur,
  Are sapped for a smile of King Gold.

Beguiled of their native demeanour,
  The high rush with heirlooms and bays
The poor with what gold cannot weigh, nor
  The skill of the pedant appraise ;
The soldier he spurs with his duty,
  And lo ! by the frenzy made bold,
The damsel she glides with her beauty,
  To garnish the brow of King Gold.

Accustomed to traffic forbidden
  By honour—by heaven—each hour,
The purest, by conscience unchidden,
  Laugh, laugh at the noble and pure ;
And Chastity, rein'd in a halter,
  Is led to the temple and sold,—
Devotion herself, at the altar,
  Yields homage alone to King Gold.

Affection on whose honey blossom,
  The child of affliction still fed—

Affection is plucked from the bosom,
  And malice implanted instead;
And dark grow the brows of the tender,
  And colder the hearts of the cold :—
Love, pity, and justice surrender
  Their charge to the hounds of King Gold.

See, see, from the sear'd earth ascending,
  A cloud o'er the welkin expands;
See, see, 'mid the dense vapour bending,
  Pale women with uplifted hands;
Smokes thus to the bridegroom of Circe,
  The dear blood of hundreds untold;
Invoke thus the angel of mercy,
  A curse on the reign of King Gold.

It sounded in castle and palace,
  It sounded in cottage and shed,
It sped over mountains and valleys,
  And withered the earth as it sped;
Like a blast in its fell consummation,
  Of all that we holy should hold,
Thrilled, thrilled thro' the nerves of the nation;
  "Cling! Clang! for the reign of King Gold."

MARY OF CROFTON.

Ah! a lovely jewel was Mary of Crofton,
  And now, she is cold in the clay,
We think of the heart-cheering image as often
  As we pass down the old waggon way.

C

Her air was a magical air, and the very
  Stone heart of the stoic entranced;
While her wee, wee feet beat a measure as merry
  As ever by damsel was danced.

Her accents enchanted; her lay—but the silly
  Bit linnet to vie it would seek;
And the rose in her hair was a daffadowndilly
  Compared with the rose on her cheek.

Sue, Bessy, and Kitty still ornament Crofton,
  And rich are the charms they display;
But we miss the sweet image of Mary as often
  As we pass down the old waggon way

ANNIE LEE.

ANNIE LEE is fair and sweet—
  Fair and sweet to look upon;
But Annie's heart is all deceit:
  Therefore Annie Lee, begone.

To conceive her smiles, conceive
  Smiles the lily's self might own;
But a snare for me they'd weave:
  Therefore Annie Lee, begone.

Sweeter than a golden bell
  Sound her winning words, each one;—
From a fount of fraud they well;
  Therefore Annie Lee, begone.

In those deep blue orbs, her eyes,
    Pity's built herself a throne ;
Pity !   Guile in Pity's guise :
    Therefore Annie Lee, begone.

Charming Annie Lee, begone !
    Cunning Annie Lee, begone !
I'd not have thee for a world,
    Tho' so fair to look upon.

THISTLE AND NETTLE.

'Twas on a night, with sleet and snow
    From out the north a tempest blew,
When Thistle to her cot did go
    The little Nettle's self to woo.

His errand known, she, with a frown,
    Up from a sock a-knitting sprung ;
Down took the broom and swept the room,
    While like a bell her clapper rung.'

" Have I not seen enough to be
    Convinced for ever soon or late
The maid shall rue the moment she
    Attendeth to a wooer's prate ?

" How long ago since Phemie Hay
    To Harry at the Mill fell wrong ?
How long since Hall a prank did play
    Shall e'er be rued by Ellen Strong ?

C 2

" How long ago since Adam Smith
   Wooed Annie on the Moor, and left
The lassie with a stain ? yea, with
   A heart of every hope bereft ?

" But what need instant cases ? lo !
   Have I not heard thee chaunt the lay
' The fraud of men was ever so
   Since summer first was leafy ? ' eh ?

" When men are to be trusted, then,
   —But never may that time befall ;
Of five times five-and-twenty men,
   There's barely five are men at all.

"Before the timid maid they'll fall,
   And smile and weep and sigh and sue ;
Till once they get her in their thrall,
   And then she's doomed her lot to rue.

" For her a subtle snare they weave,
   And when the bonny bird is theirs,
Then, then they giggle in their sleeve ;
   Then, then they laugh at all her fears.

" Another western wind, they woo
   The bloom its treasures to unfold ;
Extracts its wealth—their way pursue,
   And leaves her pining on the wold.

"—When men are men, come woo me then—
   Till then, lo I am on my guard,
And he the loon that brings me down,
   He, he'll be pardoned on my word ! "

Thus for an hour her tongue was heard,
  By this, her words grown faint and few,
She raised the broom at every word,
  And thumped the floor to prove it true.

In ardent words the youth replied :—
  " Dread hollow-heart guile thou must,
But deem not all of honour void
  Nor punish all with thy mistrust.

" A few, not all the lash have earn'd,
  Let but that few be lashed. Nay, sure,
The world were topsy-turvy turned,
  Did not some sense of right endure.

" Destroy the weed, but spare the flower ;
  Consume the chaff but keep the grain ;
Nor harry one who'd die before
  He'd give thy little finger pain."

On hearing this, she sat her down,
  Took up her needle-work again,
And tho' she strove to wear a frown,
  Made answer in a milder strain.

" Forego thy quest. Deceitful words
  May be, as they have been, may be
A fatal lure to lighter birds,
  They'll never prove the like to me.

" Still by my chastity I vow,
  As I have kept the cheat at bay,
So, should I keep my senses, so
  I'll keep him till my dying day.

" The best that man can do or say,
  The love of gold or rubies rare,
Not all that wealth can furnish, may
  Once lure to leave me in a snare.

" So end thy quest."   He only prest
  His ardent suit the more, while she
At every word he uttered, garr'd
  Her fleeing needles faster flee.

" My quest by honour's justified ;
  I long have eyed and found thee still
The maid I'd like to be my bride ;
  Would I could say the maid that will.

" Hadst thou but been a daffodil
  That with the breezes sport and play,
For all thy suitor valued, still
  Thou so hadst danced thy life away.

" But thou so fair art chaste."   Thus he
  Unto her answer answers e'er,
And that too in a way that she
  Must will or nill his answer hear.

And then a chair he'd ta'en, his chair
  Unto her chair he nearer drew ;
Recurr'd to memories sweet and rare,
  And in a softer key did woo.

He spake of moments vanished, when
  The happiest pair of all the young
They hand in hand a-down the glen
  Together sported, danced and sung.

The linnet's self the boughs among,
   The lammie skipping o'er the way,
Sang not than they, a sweeter song,
   Played not a merrier prank than they.

"Ah, these were golden times!" Thus goes
   His descant till her brow grows sleek,
Till lo! the lily drives the rose.
   The rose the lily from her cheek.

And now the iron sparking hot
   Around with might and main he swings,
And down upon the proper spot
   With bang on bang the hammer brings.

"Be, be my suit but undenied,
   And ere the moon is on the wane
A knot shall by the priest be tied,
   The priest shall never loose again.

"In heart and hand excelled by none,
   Henceforth I'd front the ills of life,
And every victory I won
   Should be a jewel for my wife

"So should the people of the dell
   When they convened to gossip say,
For harmony we bore the bell,
   And bore it with a grace away.

"Nay, lift thy head, be not ashamed
   If thus to feel—and thus—and, O!
As matters sinful might be blamed—
   Then saints were sinners long ago."

Here silence deep ensued. The cat
    That lately took the nook had stept
To mark the sequel of their chat,
    Came forth, lay on the earth, and slept.

The needles that flew here and there,
    And in their glee had sought to vie
A moon-beam dance upon the mere,
    Neglected on her apron lie.

In concord with the storm within,
    The storm without forbears to blow ;
And 'tween the sailing clouds begin
    The joyous stars to come and go.

O'er all delight prevails. Nor swayed
    By doubt and dread she longer seems,
But on our hero's bosom laid
    The maid a dream of rapture dreams.

Dream on blest maid ! An hour like this
    Annuls an age of care and strife,
And turns into a drop of bliss
    The bitter cup of human life.

The tear is by a halo gilt,
    The thorns of life are changed to flowers ;
The dirge into a merry lilt,
    When love return'd for love is ours.

And so our heroine felt. In soft
    Sweet tones, at length her accents flow—
" I've heard of honied tongues full oft,
    But never felt their force till now.

" Still would I fume as day by day
I've seen our damsels bought and sold
By some I'd scorn to own, had they
Outweighed their very weight in gold.

" My hour of triumph's o'er.   In vain
Did I my fellow maids abuse,
I've snatched the cup and drank the bane
That sets me in their very shoes.

" That turns a heart of adamant
To pliant wax ; and in my turn
Subjects me to the bitter taunt
The vanquish'd victor's ever borne.

" That leaveth Nettle satisfied
To leave her kith and kin, and by
Her ever faithful Thistle's side
To shelter till the day they die."

———

THE STARS ARE TWINKLING.

THE stars are twinkling in the sky,
As to the pit I go ;
I think not of the sheen on high,
But of the gloom below.

Not rest nor peace, but toil and strife,
  Do there the soul .enthral,
And turn the precious cup of life
  Into a cup of gall.

HEY ROBIN.

(The first two lines are old.)

Hey Robin, jolly Robin,
  Tell me how thy lady doth?
Is she laughing, is she sobbing,
  Is she gay or grave, or both?

Is she like a linnet gaily
  Lilting in her father's hall?
Or a surly steer, and daily
  Sour to each and sour to all?

Is she like a violet, breathing
  Blessings on her native place?
Or a sting-clad nettle scathing
  All who dare approach her grace?

Is she like a dew drop sparkling
  When the morn peeps o'er the land
Or a cloud the day a-darkling,
  And which bodes a storm at hand?

Tut! to count the freaks of woman,
  Count the pebbles of the seas;
Rob, thy lady's not uncommon
  Be or do she what she please!

LOVE WITHOUT HOPE.

THE glory of her charms I felt,
 And thro' my frame electric ran
What made my stubborn heart to melt,
 And feel as hearts of passion can ;
And from that hour, her eyes of jet,
 And every trait and every hue,
In her delightful being met,
 Pursues me and shall e'er pursue.

A vision bright, a form of light
 She glides before my inner eyes ;
And tho' anear she doth appear,
 In vain for her my bosom sighs—
In vain, in vain, and woe and pain
 Are mine—and woe and pain alone—
Another's arms must fold those charms,
 Which I would give a world to own.

Upon the block with nerve of rock,
 This hour would see my head reclined,
Could such this hour but me assure
 My image in her heart were shrined ;
Yes, yes, for this unequalled bliss,
 Upon the wings of rapture born,
My soul would cleave the air and leave
 Her mortal bonds asunder torn !

A niche possessed within her breast,
 Ay, more than life I'd value that—

What were it then, could I but strain
  Her to my heart my own ? ay, what ?
Entranced I feel, my senses reel,—
  Up in a fiery whirlwind caught
Away, they fly and leave me—ay,
  Half frantic at the very thought !

What would I have, what do I crave ?
  What were a sin for me to touch !—
Yon radiant star that beams from far,
  Her lustre equals twenty such ;
She's past compare a jewel rare,
  Of value more than crowns can boast ;
Whilst I who sigh—ah what am I ?
  A wretch who merits scorn at most.

Far, far above my worth and love
  Is she—and were she less divine,
Another's arms would fold her charms,
  And I were destined still to pine ;
Thus double doomed to be consumed
  By passion's raging fires, I know
On earth a hell as fierce and fell,
  As aught a future state could show.

Alas ! alas ! we seldom love
  Where love may equal love obtain ;
Our idols in our fancy move—
  Fleet phantoms we may chase in vain ;
We either love what's little worth,
  And live to rue the sequel ; or,
What never can be ours on earth,
  And so must evermore deplore !

THE STAINED LILY.

WHEN first the maiden fair I eyed,
  —*This world is a world of grief alone*—
A lily she held and a rose beside—
  But I was doomed her lot to moan.

The rose was gain'd and the lily was stain'd
  —*This world is a world of grief alone*—
And from that hour her beauty waned,
  And I was left her lot to moan.

The lily was stain'd when the rose was gain'd
  —*This world is a world of grief alone*—
And from that hour her life-star waned,
  And I was left her lot to moan.

Ah, never more in my sight she'll stand
  —*This world is a world of grief alone*—
With a lily bright in her lily-white hand,
  And I am doomed her lot to moan.

ROSA REA.

The following was suggested by a sweet little lyric, entitled
"Resolution," translated from the German of Uhland.

THE sun is in the western sky
  And thro' the barley, she—
Comes she, the apple of my eye,
  The rose-cheeked Rosa Rea.

Away I slink the maid to meet,
  As if I went away,
Alone to please a pair of feet,
  Resolved to go astray.

I whistle as I go, tho' what
  I cannot tell, but know
Right well my heart goes pit-a-pat
  With every note I blow.

Anon, I, silent as the path
  Whereon I tread become,
The power to blow my whistle, hath
  Ta'en wing and left me dumb.

The lark's loud lilt so bright and clear
  Is ringing in the sky;
A dearer tune I hear—I hear
  Two little feet draw nigh.

Two feet I hear approaching near
  —Abashed I hing my head—
Two little feet a hornpipe beat,
  Or is't my heart instead?

A floweret I of scarlet dye
  Espy as on I tread;
The maid who trips this way hath lips—
  Two lips of richer red.

A 'floweret I hard by espy,
  A gem of azure hue;
The maid who hies this way hath eyes—
  Two eyes of sweeter blue.

Those tiny blooms my heart might steal,
  Did not a spell profound
Now gar my mortal reason reel,
  Or gar the world go round.

My senses swim, my sight grows dim,
  A-near, more near her tread—
Her little feet a hornpipe beat,
  ˙ Or is't my heart instead?

Ah, am I moving on my feet?
  Or am I on my head?
Do airy dreams my senses cheat?
  Am I alive or dead?

Not dead! away, that notion, nay,
  Not in a dream I move;
Lo, in the clear bright pool I near
  I see my own dear love.

She nears—appears a blink uprears
  My head—O joy!—ah see!
Till night's o'erhead, locked hand in hand
  Stand I, and—Rosa Rea!

———

SLIGHTED.

Ah me! my heart is like to break,
The envied rose upon my cheek,
The blood-red rose is cold and bleak,
  Since he has slighted me!

Once I—the purest drop of dew,
The sweetest cherry ever grew—
Once such I seemed unto his view,
   But now he scowls at me!

Alas! a shadow lone and pale,
I all unheard my lot bewail;
He listens to another's tale—
   He has no ear for me!

Could he but look upon my grief,
Would he not try to bring relief?
I feel my days below are brief
   By his harsh ways to me!

I trail about I know not how,
I, like a thief, sink down the row,
For well behind my back I know
   The rest all laugh at me!

The rest to one another wink,
Whenever down the row I slink,—
Their hearts are fill'd with glee to think
   How he's deserted me!

The very bairns have caught their words
As notes are caught by mocking birds—
By jibes are rent my bosom chords,
   And grief is killing me!

I feel my days on earth are brief—
Ah! could he look upon my grief,
Would he not try to bring relief,
   And rue his wrong to me?

I dream'd last night to me he came,
A blush was on his cheek for shame,
He took my hand—he breathed my name,
　　And spake kind words to me !

Back from mine eyes my locks he drew,
He bound them with a ribbon blue,
And kissed me as he used to do—
　　He gave such looks to me !

Such looks ? No sun will rise nor set
When I forget those looks—forget
Those star-bright eyes—those eyes of jet
　　That stole my heart from me !

The vision fled ! and I was left
To mourn my lot with heart thrice cleft—
To mourn a lot of hope bereft,
　　By his false vows to me !

He'll rue that e'er he wronged me so,
Yet were my woe a greater woe
I would not do by him—ah, no !
　　As he has done by me !

My peace is flown, my heart is sore,
A canker eats into its core,
Yet would I breathe my last, before
　　He'd wring a curse from me !

Ah, me, my heart !—Deceiver say
How could'st thou wile my heart away,
Then leave me thus by night and day
　　To sigh and pine for thee ?

THE DEWDROP.

AH, be not vain. In yon flower-bell
  I gleamed what might a crown begem,
So many deemed who mark'd me well,
  And few did differ much from them.

Thus was it till a cruel blast
  Arose and swept me to the ground,
When in the jewel of the past
  Earth but a drop of water found.

———

THE BUTTERFLY.

THE butterfly from flower to flower
  The urchin chased ; and when at last
He caught it in my lady's bower,
  He cried, "ha, ha !" and held it fast.

Awhile he laugh'd but soon he wept
  When looking at the prize he'd caught,
He found he had to ruin swept,
  The very glory he had sought,

THE COLLIER LAD.

My lad he is a Collier Lad,
  And a blithe, blithe soul is he,
And when a holiday comes round,
  He'll spend that day in glee;
He'll tell his tale o'er a pint o' ale,
  And crack his joke, and bad
Must be the heart who loveth not
  To hear the Collier Lad.

At bowling matches on the green
  He ever takes the lead,
For none can swing his arm and fling
  With such a pith and speed;
His bowl is seen to skim the green,
  And bound as it were glad
To hear the cry o' victory
  Salute the Collier Lad.

When 'gainst the wall they play the ball,
  He's never known to lag,
But up and down he gars it bowne
  Till all his rivals fag;
When deftly,—lo! he strikes a blow
  Which gars them all look sad,
And wonder how it came to pass
  They play'd the Collier Lad.

D 2

The quoits are out, the hobs are fix'd,—
  The first round quoit he flings
Enrings the hob; and lo ! the next
  The hob again unrings ;
And thus he'll play a summer's day,
  The theme o' those who gad,
And youngsters shrink to bet their brass
  Against the Collier Lad.

When in the dance he doth advance,
  The rest all sigh to see
How he can spring and kick his heels
  When they a-wearied be ;
Your one-two-three, with either knee
  He'll beat, and then, glee mad,
A heel-o'er-head leap crowns the dance,
  Danced by the Collier Lad.

He seldom goes to church, I own,
  And when he does, why then,
He with a leer will sit and hear,
  And doubt the holy men ;
This very much annoys my heart,
  But soon as we are wed,
To please the priest, I'll do my best
  To tame my Collier Lad.

CHORUS—

There's not his match in smoky Shields—
  Newcastle never had
A lad in her famous Guilds
  To match the Collier Lad.

THE WILTED LEAF.

WILTED is the leaf, and blown
By the cold wind up and down,
That beheld thy promise fair,
Maiden with the dark-brown hair !

Shatter'd is this heart, and hurl'd
By its grief-storm thro' the world,
Since it won that promise rare,
Maiden with the dark-brown hair !

Go thy ways ! thy locks unbraid !
Thou hast but thyself betray'd,
And must e'en my pity share,
Maiden with the dark-brown hair !

THE SEER.

WOULD I could waken numbers, brighter, sweeter,
    Than is the lark's song in the cloud above,
Then would I tell you in befitting metre,
    How much the Seer is worthy of your love.

Shy, sensitive is he, and far from equal
    Unto the battle of material life,
He strives unheeded, and too oft the sequel
    Unheeded falleth in the bitter strife.

Averse to falsehood and pretences hollow,
　　Averse to slander, cruelty and wrong,
He scorns the gilded car of pomp to follow,
　　And underneath is trampled by the throng.

Too nobly strung of self to brook the mention—
　　Of aught essential to his personal gain—
Too finely strung to pleasure in contention,
　　He seeks within the peace he would obtain.

Unlike the crowd who never dare look inward,
　　Lest they a hideous spectre there should meet,
Would point to secret longings prompting sinward,
　　He looks within and finds a solace sweet.

There in a conscience pure he sees a charmer,—
　　A harper from whose harp such tones are hurl'd,
They act as mighty spells, as tested armour,
　　To shield him from the malice of the world.

"Go on brave heart," he hears an anthem chanted,
　　The distant echoes of that harp's weird tones;
"Go on—to thee a richer dower is granted
　　Than that which gilds a hundred monarchs' thrones.

"Thou may'st be thrust aside and scorned and taunted
　　As being a lunatic, a knave or fool,
Thou hast within thy inner being planted
　　A power that yet shall put the world to school.

"Thou may'st be destined here to tribulation;
　　Thy every pang shall prove a key by which
Thou shalt unlock some safe of the Creation,
　　And with its precious stores thy mind enrich.

"Illumined by that sun forever burning,
   Deep in the centre of the inner spheres,
Thou shalt be gifted with the gift of learning
   What lieth hidden from thy mortal peers.

"In every planet in the midnight heaven,—
   In every hue doth the rainbow blend,
Shalt thou perceive a lore and meaning, given
   To very few on earth to comprehend.

"The very flower upon the meadow blowing,—
   The very weed down trampled on the road,
Shall be to thee a priceless casquet, glowing
   With glories hinting of the light of God.

"In every breezelet —nay, in the commotion
   Of raging winds—in every streamlet clear,—
Nay, in the roaring of the mighty ocean,
   Shalt thou hear sounds will gladden thee to hear.

"Thus shalt thou in the Universe external,
   The Universe internal read, and so
Possess what shall be to the weal eternal
   Of earth's benighted 'habitants to know.

"The buried eons of the Past—their history,
   Still glows in characters that thou shalt read ;
And from the future thou shalt pluck its mystery,
   And point the goal to where the moments lead,

"Whatever thrills the heart with feelings precious,
   Whatever lends to cast the spirit down,
The deed delightful, or the hint pernicious
   Shall claim withal in turn thy smile or frown.

"Instruct shalt thou the erring how his error
    May yet revisit his distrest survey—
How he who is to other men a terror,
    May be a terror to himself one day.

" Remind shalt thou the soul aweary, weary
    Even with the battle thou thyself hast fought,
How thro' deep failure and thro' toil uncheery,
    Must every triumph worth his care be wrought

" Nay even at the hest of a volition
    Still to the highest purposes attuned,
Shalt thou go forth a monarch, and ambition
    And evils many with thy glance confound.

" ' Woe' black-browed guilt shall cry ; and 'woe' and
      vanish
    Despair and desolation, sisters sad ;
And for the hydra-brood thou thus shalt banish,
    Celestial Love shall make the spirit glad.

" Uplifting them by slow, yet sure gradations,
    From spheres inferne into the spheres superne
Shalt thou thus prove a boon unto the nations,
    And in return a boon divine shalt earn.

" If not in monuments of brass or marble,
    Deep in Men's spirits shall thy glory glow ;
And little ones shall of the wonders warble
    Accomplished by the wise man long ago.

" All this and more than this shall be thy guerdon,—
    The sense of having acted right ! "—So says
The happy echo of that harp's sweet burden
    A certain Seraph in his bosom plays.

And this enableth the true seer ever
 To triumph tho' he falleth, and to pray
That theirs like his may be a portion, never,
 Who plot and plan to take his life away.

Ah, to the last his words and deeds are sweeter
 Than is the lark's song in the cloud above,
And rare the bard could find befitting metre,
 To hymn the love we owe this child of Love!

THE MYSTIC LYRE.

HEAVEN-GIFTED was the mortal, thrice-illum'ed by
 heaven's own fire,
 A bard the cords of whose great soul to love and truth
 were strung,
Who deemed the mighty universe itself a seven-stringed
 lyre
 From which at the Creator's touch the anthem, Life, is
 wrung.

An instrument it is by which a gamut vast is spann'd,
 Whose every tone's in unison with every other tone;
And which alone is given to the heart to understand
 Who to pity gives an ear of soul—to self an ear of
 stone.

To such a one the accents of that magic lyre expound
 The kinship of all beings great and small, and how the
 sweet
Yet mighty octave to the key struck in yon planet's found
 Within the little dew-drop that sparkles at our feet.

In the seeming great the little, in the seeming small the
 great,
 Are render'd by that music to the pure in spirit, plain ;
And the thistle's and the lily's and the mourn'd and
 envied state,
 Are but altos and contraltos in one bright harmonic
  strain.

In the seeming ill the good is, in the seeming good the ill ;
 But in Life's complex measure what the ill deplored
  appears,
Is often but a needful step into a varied trill
 That terminates with rapture what began 'mid doubts
  and fears.

All height and depth of moral being are compass'd in
 one chant,
 And thro' vast scales descending in the lowest soul is
  heard
True echoes, true, tho' faint, of what the highest soul can
 vaunt,
 Whilst to the lowest full as oft the highest yields
  a chord.

The measure of the man with all his destiny so vast,
 When the key-note of the living known is stricken
  may be shown ;
And the burden of the future and the burden of the past,
 Are but coloured octaves to the note from out the
  present thrown.

The measure of the angel in the measure of the man,
 Yea, he the highest seraph in the lowest serf's
  conceal'd ;
And the diapason struck on earth compriseth in its span,
 An echo of the heaven itself in angel-states reveal'd.

Not that which was, is that which is, as sang the
  Hebrew sage,
  But a duller to a brighter chord ; and that which is, in
    turn,
Is but a stage in life's great march prophetic of a stage
  That awaits the soul's arrival when we leap death's
    dreaded burn.

The mighty universe itself is but a mighty lyre,
  From which at the Creator's touch the anthem, Life,
    is flung ;
And could we heed its music up would leap our souls on
    fire,
  And up a hymn to Love Eterne would leap from
    every tongue !

THE SPELL.

" LOVE's a pleasure, love's a treasure,
    Why the joys of love withstand ? "
  Alf so pleadeth, Effie heedeth
    And—What ails the lily-wand ?

Lighter grow her airs and lighter—
    Glances she would shun she seeks ;
  Brighter burn her eyes, and brighter
    Burns the scarlet on her cheeks.

Leaps her heart within her ; cheerly
  Smiles the earth in silence girt ;
Dance the stars above, and rarely,
  All in concord with her heart.

Redder than the red rose blowing
  Sinks she in her wooer's arms ;
Many a mad, mad vow avowing
  Melt they in each other's charms.

For a season vanished reason—
  Vanished to return and view
Loved and lover—and for ever—
  Doom'd the spell of love to rue.

————

THE FIXT STAR.

DIRECTED by a little star,
  I paced towards my own loved cot,
When rushed a meteor from afar,
  And I my little guide forgot.

Bedazzled was I, and amazed,
  When out the meteor flashed, and I
Had never more my threshold paced,
  Had not that star still gleamed on high.

WILLY TO JINNY.

DUSKIER than the clouds that lie
' Tween the coal-pit and the sky,
Lo, how Willy whistles by   •
    Right cheery from the colliree.

Duskier might the laddie be
Save his coaxing coal-black e'e,
Nothing dark could Jinny see
    A-comming from the colliree.

MOTHER WEPT.

MOTHER wept, and father sighed ;
    With delight a-glow
Cried the lad, " to-morrow," cried,
    " To the pit I go."

Up and down the place he sped,—
    Greeted old and young,
Far and wide the tidings spread,
    Clapt his hands and sung.

Came his cronies some to gaze
    Wrapt in wonder ; some
Free with counsel ; some with praise ;
    Some with envy dumb.

" May he," many a gossip cried,
" Be from peril kept ;"
Father hid his face and sighed,
Mother turned and wept.

ARACHNE.

I READ in an old book the myth
Of the Hellenian damsel with
The magic needle, when there fell
On me a power—a mystic spell—
I could not well to others tell,
But all at once my soul was swept
Into a sphere where sorrow kept
Her vigils sad.   There on my ear
Awoke in accents deep, yet clear,
What might in my weak English to
A sympathetic ear thus flow :—

" The guerdon of my heavy sin
Forever thus I toil and spin
The fatal cord, the lash accursed,
By which my heavy woe is nursed."

" From whence this wail?" I inly asked,
When thro' the gloom I saw unmasked
One, from whose thin wan face and look,
I for the needle-worker took ;

And lifting up my voice I said :—
" And art thou she of whom I've read—
Arachne's self?   No answer made
The image pale, nor turned, nor fled,
Nor into air, thin air dissolved.:
But while within my thoughts revolved,
A something on my vision loom'd,
Tho' what it was might be presumed
Not clearly seen, at least by one,
Still bound to earth by flesh and bone ;
But whatsoe'er it was or meant,
Anon thereon her gaze was bent,
And this way that, her white hands went,
Whilst to their motion keeping time,
Re-woke upon my ear the chime,
Which might in my weak English to
A sympathetic ear thus flow ;—

" The guerdon of my ebon sin,
Forever thus I toil and spin,
The fatal cord, the lash accursed,
By which my heavy woe is nursed.

" The sun and moon, they come and go,
The ocean's waters ebb and flow ;
My baleful star must even burn,
My swollen tide know no return.

"Woe, woe the day, woe, woe the day
I first did feel that piercing ray,
Beneath whose magic touch, behold,
The rock's converted into gold.

" Ah, from that hour did earth become
To me a glad, a jewell'd home ;
Where-e'er I turned enrapt I viewed,
A living fact the fair and good.

" Where-e'er I turned enrapt I viewed,
A living fact the fair and good,
Which to my spirit's chambers sped,
And with the inner beauty wed.

" As casquets in which gems are shrined,
So from the lustre of my mind,
My body borrowed splendour, till
My presence stood a living will.

" Entranced I took the web and wrought
A vision so with beauty fraught,
The gazer held his breath and crept
Into himself, and smiled and wept.

" Delusive tears, delusive smiles,
What were you but the serpent's toils ?—
The nectar sparkling in yon cup,
To writhe the lips that quaff it up ?

" Flushed with success I then did cast,
A scornful glance upon the past,
And from that moment I began
A course which ended in this ban.

" The very God within me burns ;
My soul a mortal triumph spurns ;
Not mortals, o'er immortals must
I stride, or perish in the dust.

" Thus frantically cried I, when
Was flashed upon my inner ken
Minerva's might and sheen, and I,—
What was there left me but to die ?

" A meteor in the night, her might
And sheen is flashed upon my sight ;
But as the night by meteor cleft,
My soul again in gloom is left.

" I view the den in which I crawl,
I view what doth my soul appal ;
But ah, ere I my plight can mend,
All hope to me hath found an end.

" And now instead of sylvan ground,
Where grief was lost, where joy was found ;
My path is such each step I take,
Awakes the hissing of the snake.

" My night is still by horrors throng'd,
My day is but that night prolong'd ;
The sun may set, the sun may rise,
No soothing slumber seals my eyes.

" Around, beneath, and over-head,
The finger of the Livine Dread
Has fix'd a curse which see—What's this
Would thus o'er-brim my heart with bliss ?

" Yes, yes my hand that vision traced,
Mine ivory brow with wreaths are graced ;
Aloud my pean's sung, aloud,
And she my rival's head down bowed.

E

" No, never since the world begun,
Was ever such a triumph won
By mortal or immortal—nay—
I've brook'd the worst an earth-born may.

" The sun and moon they come and go,
The ocean's waters ebb and flow,
My baleful star must ever burn,
My swollen tide know no return.

"And, such the guerdon of my sin
Thus, thus to toil, and thus to spin
The fatal cord, the lash accursed,
By which my heavy woe is nursed."

Thus mourned the damsel ; while she mourn'd
Back into sense my soul return'd ;
At which receded from my sight
The needle-worker's image.   Light
Was breaking in the orient, yet,
Not till again the sun had set,
Could I forget her wail—nor then,
Nay, even till this, the strain,—
" The guerdon of my heavy sin
Forever thus I toil and spin,"
Will break upon my inner ear
And down my cheek will steal a tear,
For one whom Fame in days of old
Crowned with her brightest wreath, and bold,
And brave, and wise, alike proclaimed
The glory of that gift which framed
What their own triumphs shamed.

A LULLABY.

(Based on an Old Verse.)

THRO' the dark and dreary night,
  Golden slumbers kiss thine eyes ;
Sleep, and in the early light
  With a golden smile arise !
    Sleep, my baby, do not cry
    —Lulla, lulla, lullaby.

Trouble art thou ? baby, nay ;
  Brightest star in all my sky,
Since was turned to night my day,
  And thy father—Do not cry !
    Sleep, my baby, do not cry
    —Lulla, lulla, lullaby.

The round red moon, she's sinking low ;
  The wind up-tears the very roof ;—
The moon may sink, the wind may blow
  For thee, my child, I'm tempest proof !
    Sleep, my baby, do not cry
    —Lulla, lulla, lullaby.

WILLY TO LILY.

MUST all the passion which I've strove
  So long to hide be paid with scorn ?
And must a bosom framed for love,
  Be doomed a hopeless love to mourn ?

E 2

And must thou still its homage spurn?
  And must thou still my suit reject?
And be to me this cruel thorn?
  Reflect upon the past, reflect!

A time there was and time shall pass
  To me ere that forgotten be,
When side by side from tide to tide
  We played and sported on the lea.

Then, then have I not chased the bee
  From bloom to bloom—oft chased and caught,
And having drawn its sting in glee,
  To thee the little body brought?

Then, when a bloom of rarer dyes
  Into my busy fingers fell,
To whom was reached the lucky prize?
  Can not thy recollection tell?

As oft away as summer went,
  Who pulled with thee the haw, bright, brown—
Brown as thy own bright eyes—and bent
  For thee the richest branches down?

With blooms I've graced thy yellow hair,
  With berries filled thy lap—thy hand,—
That hand as alabaster fair—
  Had every gift at my command.

Nay, tho' to others dour, yet meek
  I ever was to thee, and kind,
And when we played at hide and seek,
  I hid where thou would'st seek to find.

Upon the play-ground still unmatched
  Was I, unless my Lily played;
And then it seem'd to those who watched,
  My failures were on purpose made.

As sure as e'er a race began,
  The palm was mine unless she joined,
And then I always was out-ran
  For still with her I lagged behind.

The ball I knocked to others mocked
  Their efforts to arrest its flight;
But when my ball to her was knocked,
  It would upon her lap alight.

None, up and down so well I bobbed,
  To skip the rope with me would try,
Did she attempt? my skill was robbed;
  Another skipped her out—not I.

At play thus was't but childhood past,
  And e'er the lasses reached their teens,
Atween them and the lads a vast
  Mysterious distance intervenes.

They seldom on the green appear
  In careless sport and play; and if
They join the throng erect they wear
  Their head and still their air is stiff—

They ail they know not what. And such
  The change that on my lassie fell;
Then would she shrink my hand to touch,
  And I have feared her touch as well.

Had I changed too? This I can tell,
  That touch o'er me a spell would cast,
And did I pass her in the dell
  With slow and snail-like pace I pass'd.

Her voice had lost its former ring;
  Yet in that voice such power was flung,
I better liked to hear her sing
  Than when of old to me she sung.

Her touch, her tone, would make or mar
  My bliss, and tho' with all my skill
I strove to please and please but her,
  I in her presence blundered still.

When by the hearth she sewing sat,
  Did I to thread her needle try
Still, still my heart played pit-a-pat,
  And still I missed the needle's eye.

As with the needle-threading, so
  We with the skein-a-winding fared,
And Auntie's dreaded tongue would go
  Before the dancing end appeared.

" What ails the lass?" she often said;
  " She's sound asleep!" once said, and flew
And snatched and snapped the tangled thread;
  Whilst I, I know not how, withdrew.

Away too fled those hours!—Alack!
  They came and went like visions rare,
To mock the heart, delude, and wrack,
  And leave the gazer in despair.

Ah, less—tho' sun-illum'ed—less fair
  The bubbles dancing down the burn :
And let them burst, they'll re-appear
  Ere those delightsome hours return.

But they may live in thought ; and could
  They live in Lily's thought again,
Would she not change her bearing ? would—
  Would she not change her bitter strain ?

Would she her Willy still disdain ?
  Would she continue thus to gall
And put me to this cruel pain ?
  Recall to mind the past, re-call !

POLITICAL VACILLATION.

(1868.)

Now Gladstone's party bears the bell,
  And now Disraeli's—now
The people really cannot tell,
  For whom their hands to show.

Now this way, la, now that inclined,
  A giddy vane they go,
The victim of each puff of wind
  The demagogues may blow.

THE HELL BROTH.

The devil and the devil's brood
  Around a boiling caldron hung,
While in a nook in merry mood
  Grim Death a dainty ditty sung ;
For guided by a baleful star
  The devil himself had caused to beam,
Lo, myriads hurried from afar
  To reap the fruit of a darksome dream :
On, on they came with cheek a-flame
  And lips that quivered as they sought
In tones subdued the demon brood,
  For but a drop of the magic pot.
—Anon around was the hell-broth spun,
  And a measure brimmed to old and young,
The while delighted with the fun,
  Grim Death a dainty ditty sung.

That potion quaft, in his conceit
  Behold the dwarf a giant tread,
At least a hundred thousand feet
  Above his worthier neighbour's head ;
Despising still or lord or serf,
  About the land he strutting goes,
'Till bang against a brother dwarf,
  The merry fellow runs his nose :—
Thus many a one—loon, fop, and clown—
  A lesson to their sorrow got,
And yet aloud they pray the brood
  For deeper draughts of the magic pot.
—Anon around was the hell-broth spun,
  And a measure drained by old and young,
The while delighted with the fun,
  Grim Death a dainty ditty sung.

Now double-drugg'd the rout about
  A soul-consuming furnace bore,
And what they took to put it out,
  But only made it burn the more :
It burnt in heart, it burnt in brain,
  And from its fumes arose a sprite,
One, whom her favours to obtain
  They chased by day, they chased by night ;
And still as they deemed her their prey,
  Away, away with a leer she shot,
'Mid cries right loud to the demon brood,
  For deeper draughts of the magic pot.
—Again around was the hell-broth spun,
  And a measure drained by old and young,
The while delighted with the fun,
  Grim Death a daintier ditty sung.

So la, ta, la !—that fiery draught
  Now led them one and all a dance :
Lo, ere the drug was wholly quaft,
  Each threw on each a lurid glance ;
And from that glance a wasp took wing,
  From busy tongue to ear it flew,
And ever around it bore a sting
  The devil himself had cause to rue :
It stung them black, it stung them blue,
  And with each sting the louder got
Their cries right loud to the demon brood,
  For deeper draughts of the magic pot.
—Again around was the hell-broth spun,
  And a measure drained by old and young,
The while delighted with the fun,
  Grim Death a daintier ditty sung.

That horrid draught being duly quaft,
    A cry o'er plain and mountain rolled,
At which the strong the weaker took,
    And bartered body and soul for gold :
And of the gold thus gotten they
    At once a gloomy castle built
Whose dome might from the eye of day
    Forever hide their horrid guilt :
Tombed in their victims' blood-price thus,
    Long revelled they and faltered not
To cry aloud to the demon brood,
    For deeper draughts of the magic pot.
—But around no more was the hell-broth spun ;
    Awe-struck the fiends in the pot had sprung,
The while surfeited with the fun,
    Death cursed the dainty lay he'd sung.

—————

THE TOAST.

I'M as loyal a subject as Britain can boast,
    Our Queen she is gracious, and gentle, and wise ;
But another this moment demandeth my toast,—
    'Tis Annie, the lass with the two hazel eyes.

The hair of my idol's a stream of delight,
    The lustre thereof with the aerolite vies ;
Her dimpled cheeks apples, the pure red and white,
    But these are outshone by her two hazel eyes.

Her breasts are two hillocks of new-driven snow,
　Between them a dell of enchantment lies,
Where love lurks, the elf! with his death-darts, but no—
　These cannot be named with her two hazel eyes.

The golden-eyed lily's a type of the grace
　Combined in her form, her demeanour, and guise ;
A jewel is she in heart, language, and ways,
　But nothing can equal her two hazel eyes.

I'm as loyal a subject as Britain can boast ;
　Victoria's gentle, gracious, and wise ;
But another this moment demandeth my toast,—
　I drink to the lass with the two hazel eyes

TWO HAZEL EYES.

Was ever a bard in such pitiful plight?
　Was ever such seen by yon stars in the skies?
A-pit or a-bed—by day and by night,
　I'm plagued by the magic of two hazel eyes.

A leaf in a whirlwind, I'm sent to and fro,
　And peace, panic-stricken, my bosom still flies ;
For rest I implore, but my portion below
　Is the rest-killing magic of two hazel eyes.

The world it goes up, and the world it goes down,
　And the lofty descend, and the lowly arise ;
But fortune, the jilter, may smile or may frown,
　I feel but the magic of two hazel eyes.

Once blithe as a linnet I lilted my lay,
  And won the applause of both foolish and wise—
Now deaf, dumb, derided, I go on my way,
  Bewitched by the magic of two hazel eyes.

O Annie, wouldst thou but look down on my plight,
  And pity my case, and no longer despise,
I'd dance in delight, I'd sing day and night,
  And the theme of my lays be thy two hazel eyes !

———

THE SEATON TERRACE LASS.

My love at Seaton Terrace dwells,
  A hale and hearty wight,
Who lilts away the summer day,
  Also the winter night ;
The merriest bird with rapture stirr'd,
  Could never yet surpass
The melody awaken'd by
  The Seaton Terrace lass !

She's graceful as a lily-wand,
  Right modest too is she,
And then ye'll search in vain the land
  To find a busier bee ;
Like silver clear her iron gear
  Like burnished gold, the brass—
For tidyness there's none to peer
  The Seaton Terrace lass.

More restless than a clucking hen
  About her, Minnie stirs ;
" Go, jewel, knit your fancy net,
  And I will scour the floors."
" Enjoy the day, a-down the way,
  Where greenest grows the grass,
No help I need," replies with speed
  The Seaton Terrace lass.

She'll knit or sew, she'll bake or brew—
  She'll wash the clothes so clean,
The very daisy pales beside
  Her linen on the green ;
Then what she'll do, with ease she'll do,
  And still her manner has   ·
A charm, would gar a stoic woo
  The Seaton Terrace lass.

Discomfort flies her dark brown eyes,
  And when the men folk come
All black and weary from the pit,
  They find a welcome home.
Her brothers tease her, and a pride,
  The father feeleth as
Again he meets again he greets
  The Seaton Terrace lass.

When day is past and night at last
  Begins to cloud the dell,
She'll take her skiel and out she'll steal,
  And meet me at the well ;
Then, oh ! how fleet the moments sweet—
  Yet fleeter shall they pass,
That night the Bebside laddie weds
  The Seaton Terrace lass.

THE PROUD ONE'S DOOM.

"QUEEN PEARL'S own equal—nay,
  A fairer far am I," May Dewdrop said,
As Sol at break of day
  Did kiss the sparkler on her grass-blade bed.

"None may my charms resist!"
  "None," Sol still kissing answered; when alas!
The proud one turned to mist,
  And with her pride did into Lethe pass.

BALOO.

BALOO, my sweet baby—the blossom!—
  I dandle't till weary and sigh,
With not a bare drop in my bosom
  To silence its pitiful cry.

The red moon above us right rarely,
  I lay on the brink of the burn,
And drank in the words which so early
  Have brought me to anguish and scorn

His praises my vanity flattered,
  His vows kindled hopes which, alas!
Were fated ere long to be scattered,
  Like blobs the wind sweeps from the grass.

And had he but thought on the trouble,
  And had he but thought on the pain ;
Tho' green in the blade with the stubble,
  I'm fated to bleach on the plain.

Mid all our wooed maiden so many,
  The bonny bright lily was I ;
But now plucked and tainted, like any
  Vile weed on the footway I lie.

But let anguish thus my heart rend, and
  The briny tear thus my cheek lave ;
The longest lane yet has an end, and
  The weary sleep sound in the grave.

Baloo, my sweet baby—the blossom !—
  Ah ! hush—ere his life-glass is run,
The false one shall find in his bosom
  A pang for the deed he has done.

THE QUESTION.

WHAT can he ail ? I hear them ask ;
  And what can make his cheek so pale ?
Ah, that to answer were a task
  For which no effort could avail.
To say I love were but to say
  What many another might as well,
Who never felt the cruel sway,
  Which makes my heart with sorrow swell.

Dear are the pains of love and sweet,
   Yet he who loves, and loves in vain,
Endures a torment more complete
   Than any love-unsweeten'd pain,
Nay, keener than the savage fangs,
   Which limb from limb their victim tear,
And much more cruel are the pangs
   Which drive a lover to despair.

With feelings racked, without a spark
   Of hope to give those feelings rest,
The darksome grave is not so dark
   As is the chaos in his breast:
The brightest hour that comes and goes,
   Might just as well be dull as bright,
His grief o'er all a shadow throws,
   That hides the splendour from his sight.

Unmoved he eyes the sun arise,
   Yea, doth without a thrill behold
The sun down go at ev'ning, tho'
   He settle in a sea of gold :
The sweetest flower of field or bower,
   The brightest star by night revealed,
To him's not rare, nor sweet, nor fair,
   For him no joyous beam can yield.

The tempest swells and roars and yells,
   Up-tears and heaves to earth the oak ;
The death-bolts crash, the lightnings flash,
   And cities wrap in flame and smoke :

Let thunder crash, and lightnings flash,
   And bid him perish as they can ;
The storm he hears no death-dart bears,
   Like that which makes his life a ban.

O'er all he sees, o'er all he hears,
   The raven shades of woe are cast ;
And all his hopes, delights, and fears,
   Are now but phantoms of the past ;
The past, the present, future—all,
   All now have faded from him—ay,
All save the feeling of a thrall
   He finds he never can destroy.

He wanders wide of human haunts,
   What others do he little recks ;
Their very sympathy or taunts,
   Can little soothe, can little vex ;
Where-e'er he moves, where-e'er he turns,
   One, but one image meets his ken ;
For that he yearns and pines and mourns,
   And yearns and mourns for that in vain.

Away ! away with questions, which
   No mortal yet could answer—nay,
My pangs are far beyond the pitch
   Of seraph-tongue or pen to say ;
To speak of love were but to speak
   Of what another might, whose heart
Was never forced like mine to break,
   Yet while it breaks to hide the smart !

F

WHAT THE SIBYL SAID.

THE vision will vanish for ever,
  That gildeth this moment thy track;
And in vain were the noblest endeavour
  To call the enchantment back.

Yet pine not; a balm—an ovation
  Is thine in the thought that the day
Will come when thy bleak desolation
  Will pass like thy vision away.

THE ANGEL MOTHER.

I HAD a vision of the dear departed,
  The while stone-dead to outer things I lay;
And "Go," she said—" and tell the broken-hearted,
  What now my will shall to thy mind convey.

" I've passed the portals I so often dreaded,
  And by the fiery trial unconsumed
I find myself to life, not death, yet wedded—
  Even I whose relics you beheld entombed.

" To me the baubles of the world have vanished,
  Even with the garments I behind have left;
But not one treasure from my heart is banished,
  Not of one golden hope am I bereft.

"The self-same soul am I, the self-same being
  In every human faculty the same,
Save with a clearer, keener sense of seeing
  What path to glory leads, and what to shame.

" The wife's devotion and affection tender,—
  The mother's sweet solicitude and all
That did our home a thing of beauty render,
  Is mine, or haunts me still, and ever shall.

" Even from my sphere beyond your sphere located,
  I'm oft permitted to return—return !
To seek the halls my change left desolated,—
  To bless the dear ones left that change to mourn.

" I see the brave man by the hearth-stone sitting,
  To whom my being was and yet is wed,
I see the past before his vision flitting,—
  I see the tear-drops for his lost one shed.

" Not void of hope the dust he saw enshrouded,
  Itself was but a cerement to a soul,
Whose vision never could by death be clouded—
  He yet hath sorrows he may not control.

Full often o'er the welkin of his vision
  I see an ebon cloudlet stealing, when
A sigh is utter'd lest his hope, elysian,
  Is but a phantom of the minds of men.

" Upon my knees, unseen, before him kneeling
  I gaze into those eyes tear-blinded, till
A sense of sadness yieldeth to a feeling
  As sweet as ever did a bosom thrill.

"I point the images of those yet living,
    —Thus speak I still as I when with you spake—
When from the past into the present driven,
    His heart is up and toiling for their sake.

" 'Even for my girl,' he cries, ' so bright and airy,—
    Even for my little boy just lisping, I
Must try this death-bell monotone to vary,
    And on life's harp awake life's battle cry.'

" As he resolveth even so he doeth,
    And all the little I can do, I do
To help him to the object he pursueth,
    Or open vistas brighter to his view.

" I cannot wash as wont our jewels faces,—
    I cannot comb as wont their golden hair ;
But I can lock them in my fond embraces,
    And I can gild their minds with fancies rare.

" I cannot fetch the lisper sweet his rattle,
    Nor for the other the piano ring ;
But I can aid my boy-child in his prattle,
    And I can prompt my girl-child how to sing.

" I cannot lead them to the daisied meadows,
    But I can over-look them when they're there ;
And give a golden glow to passing shadows,
    And make the fair sunshine to them more fair.

" I cannot give them gruel in the even,
    Nor on the morn to them their toast convey ;
But when they kneel before the Lord of heaven,
    Them I can prompt for what and how to pray.

" Ay, tho' they cannot see or hear me, ever
  Into the soul of babe and father flows
The presence of their mourn'd one like a river,
  That wakens music where-so-e'er it goes.

" So, as by those the idols of my bosom,—
  Touch'd by the carol of the unseen bird ;
Touch'd by the perfume of the unseen blossom,
  The hearts of others to their depths are stirr'd.

" Nay, by each spirit sweet with whom my spirit
  In state harmonic moved and breathed, I'm felt ;
And still alive to every form of merit,
  Still dwells my love with those with whom it dwelt.

" Alive to these—to each high aspiration—
  To every base-born passion yet alive ;
To all that tendeth to man's elevation,—
  To all that downward doth the spirit drive.

" Alive to all most worthy to be cherish'd,
  Alive to all should most excite our dread ;
And being thus albeit the body's perish'd,
  How can it be averr'd that I am dead ? "

MUSIC.

I LISTEN to the accents of the silver corded harp,
  And tho' aweary of the darts at me by malice hurl'd
Aflying goes life's shuttle and aflying woof and warp --
  A renovated soul I seek to renovate the world.

As spring is to the brooklet bound in winter's icy chain,
  As showers are to the blossoms parch'd by summer's
    hottest breath ;
As sleep is to the body bow'd by toil and rack'd by pain,
  So is music to this heart to whom the jars of life are
    death.

The bonds in which I'm bound are broken by its magic
    power,
  And pent up founts of feeling flow in looks and acts
    that please ;
And refreshened as the lily is refreshened by the shower,
  The soul from trouble freed in turn the frame from
    trouble frees.

Nay, not alone from trouble freed—alone by pleasure
    fill'd—
  Not alone to strength of body and to peace of mind
    restored ;
I'm thrill'd and by a feeling that the ancients may have
    thrill'd
  When they sang the golden truths and taught what
    later times ignored.

Taught by the glamour under which I labour bright and
    clear,
  Become to me the darkest legends of an elder day ;
And so-called myths thus said or sung by bards
    illumined, wear
  The colours which the True itself and not the False
    array.

'Tis said that to the Amphionic song, sun-like, up-rose
  The Hundred-Gated City, and howe'er this be I know
At music's touch a tower-girt citadel my spirit glows,
  Thro' whose illumined corridors no hydra-doubt may go.

Not mine to under-go what under-went Arion, yet
From out a darker sea, the waters of affliction caught,
And on a brighter than a Tenarian shore I'm set
To marvel at the miracle a melody has wrought.

Not mine Orpheus like the gift to strike the lyre and
chant
What from another Pluto had another captive
charmed ;
But mine to know a lesser gift has made despair to grant
What Pluto's gruesome regions had a place of pleasure
form'd.

Nay, not a feeler merely but an actor keen am I,
Empower'd to seize the harp of life and from its cords
to bring
An anthem such as had compelled Apollo's self to sigh,
And wrung from him the palm Marsyas tried in vain
to wring.

Away into the regions of delight and, what is more,
Away into the regions of the inner life I'm borne
To learn how Nature at one birth both light and music
bore,
And how the planets danced and sung upon Creation's
morn.

At this the giddy world may laugh; their jibes are
spent in vain,—   ·
I stand above and far above the arrows at me flung :—
So chant I music-fired—and whatever worth my strain,
For men of brain, not stocks and stones, and men
of soul 'tis sung.

THE THEFT.

PERFIDIOUS damsel, with thy dazzling eyes,
Those skill'd enchanters of a sunnier clime,
Thou, thou hast charmed the dragon Reason, couched
Before my soul's Hesperides, and filched
Her fruit of burnished ore—the source itself
From which her splendour sprung—her will, and left—
Yea, naked left her to the winds of woe :
And now, while she laments her jewels lost,
With scorn dost hie to mock, to drive afar.
The veriest promise of a summer, would
Again enable her to smile, and with
Her golden apples set the world agape.

UNDECEIVED.

SECURE within his citadel, my heart,
A roystering King, has quaft his goblets brimm'd
At Pleasure's sparkling fount,—has quaft and slept ;
Has hugg'd the phantom of delight—and slept ;
Not dreaming from his sleep he'd e'er awake
To find his towers a ruin, and his bliss
Sepulchred in the dust : but now, alas !
The truth discover'd, he assumes his staff
And walks the world, and when he'd halt, lest he
Should build another citadel, and play
The merry fool he played—a voice exclaims :
" Reflect !—the Earthquake !" and he halteth not.

POOR ROSE.

" BEWARE ! yon bird now in glee on the bough
　　May drop into a snare : "
So sung we when a day of the past had passed away
　　But not when Alf. was near.

Not Cilla, not I, nor Bessy need sigh,
　　That ever he came this way ;
But a worthier far than Cilla and her
　　Has rued that evil day.

That hour the dire ban of Rosa began,
　　When Alf. glode over the hill,
And hailed us each with a blink did reach,
　　And make our heart-strings thrill.

At the brook we stoop'd, and the water scoop'd,
　　Our clean green pails into ;
When a coal-black rook beclouded the brook,
　　And away o'er the hill-top flew.

We startled, raised our heads and gazed—
　　And ere the bird had swept
From sight, heart-light, with his blink so bright,
　　The youth the waters lept.

I felt his spell, and Bessy as well,
　　As in her heart she knows ;
But Rose—did she look at her face in the brook,
　　Or why in the brook look'd Rose ?

The fact was bared, when the bird ensnared,
   Was the village talk indeed;
But he, the youth, had the look of truth—
   And who the heart can read?

Not Cilla; no—not even so—
   Not Bessy more than Cill,
Tho' she tost head in pride, and said
   What Rose remembers still.

" I think of the glance that made your hearts dance;
   But ever I think also
Of the grim black rook that darkened the brook,
   And away o'er the hill did go."

" Nay, Bessy, nay—and forbear, I pray,
   By any cold remark,
To deepen the shade that hangs o'er her head,
   If Rosa's weird be dark.

" 'The wilyest bird, on hedge ever heard '—
   Ah, well you know the rest;
The stranger youth had the look of truth—
   And looks deceive the best.

" If love-mad driven poor Rose hath given,
   What to give is woe to her,
Another more wild had been beguiled
   By lure less dazzling far."

At my sharp reply did a fierce red dye
   Bemantle Bessy's cheek,
While Rose turned as pale as the moon o'er the dale,
   But never a word did speak.

With a downcast look her needles she took,
   Till off our neighbour went,
When my hand she took and gave me a look,
   Which worlds of meaning meant.

Her tears out-gushed—in my arms she rushed,
   And kissed her Cilla, and said
What never shall pass these lips till the grass
   Is green above my head.

But oft since then, and ever when,
   I think of Rose and her ban,
Will the sad, sad strain awake in my brain,
   By which this ditty began.

" Beware, yon bird now in glee on the bough,
   May drop into a snare ! "
Alas, even so will the old thing go,
   But when will the best beware ?

———

THE OUTCAST FLOWER.

You turn up your nose at me, I suppose,
   I'm noisome and base ?
Before on my head you cruelly tread,
   Give ear to my case.

A lily-bell rare, my charms were laid bare,
   And lo ! at the sight,
In a mantle of gold, a delight to behold,
   Love danced in delight.

To him I was dear—ah me ! it was clear
      That nothing above,
Below or around, by Love could be found,
      So precious to love.

That little white flower which gildeth the hour
      When March winds rave,
The snowdrop as clear from stain might appear,
      But look'd too grave.

The crocus a-drest in her sun-given vest,
      On Spring's live mould,
To her heart's delight might sparkle as bright,
      But look'd too bold.

No zephyr did woo a hyacinth blue,
      With bearing so fine.
No daffodil e'er did view in the mere
      A face so divine.

The tulip was rich in tints, might bewitch
      A snail at his meal ;
But where the sweet smell ?—could any one tell ?—
      The dancer did feel ?

The pink had a bloom as rich in perfume,
      To make the heart glad ;
But where was the grace to rivet the gaze
      The lily-bell had ?

Not even the rose, the richest that blows,
      Could Love then prefer,
And the pansy so sweet bowed down at her feet,
      In homage to her.

This swore Love, and, sworn, away I was torn,
　　His pleasure to be ;
But ere a day past away I was cast—
　　He cared not for me.

Unheeded I pined, my sweets did the wind
　　No longer perfume ;
To vile turned the pure—the sweet turned a sour—
　　Ah, such was my doom.

You turn up your nose ! just think of my woes,
　　Though base to behold,
Just think ere you tread—ere you crush my poor head—
　　Just think what I've told

———

POLLY AND HARRY.

MERRY, lark-like, merry,
　　At the break of day,
Polly meeteth Harry
　　Coming down the way ;
And her lips, they quiver,
When her eyes discover
Smiles that speak—ah never !—
　　Peace unto the May.

Merry, blythe and merry,
　　'Neath the noontide ray,
Polly meeteth Harry
　　Coming up the way ;
And with heart a-flutter,
Seeks in vain to mutter,
What he'd have her utter—
　　What her eyes convey.

Merry, still so merry,
   At the close of day,
Polly spyeth Harry
   Wooing Ely Gray!
And when this she spyeth,
Lo! her reason dieth,
And her heart rent, cryeth
   "Woe, and well-a-day!"

———

THE CHARMER.

A SONG in devotion I sing to my Annie.
   Ah! be startled not to discover I long
To fold in my arms and possess what so many
   And many a time is the theme of my song.

My manhood's dissolved at the sight of thy beauty,
   And while heart can feel and such beauty is known,
What youth could be kept by a mere sense of duty
   From yearning to call the enchanter his own?

The saint he may blame—so to do is the fashion—
   And carp at my feelings and call them a sin,
Could beauty like thine be the price of his passion,
   He'd rush to perdition the jewel to win.

To view thy locks blacker than coal and thy glances;
   To hear thy voice, sweetest of music—ay, ay—
Thy manifold beauty my spirit entrances,
   And reason deserts me when Annie is nigh!

NIL DESPERANDUM.

WHY thus mourn o'er star-hope faded?
They are only from thy ken
By a passing vapor shaded,
And will soon appear again.
Up, and guard thee like a warrior;
Up, and make the present thine;
Trust me, every doubt's a barrier,
To Life's heritage divine.

See yon kingly soul attended
By the dulcet tones of love,
An immortal here descended,
But to lift our eyes above.
Dark as be thy lot and cruel,
He has known as dire a woe;
Bright as be his prize, a jewel
Brighter still for thee may glow.

Not the Cytherean, truly,
Vain its pursuit and unwise,
But the joy Uranian duly
Seek we that and, rich the prize.
But for that be our endeavour,
And afar our doubt and fear;
We shall then be losers never,
Tho' but losers we appear.

Tho' by many foes encircled
   Is the outer life the worst,
By whose shadow Life is darkeled
   In the heart is hatched and nursed.
All the ill to man else rendered
   Is but as a merry jest,
When compared to what's engendered
   In the soul by self possessed.

Lose we may the husk, and perish
   What the outer senses prize ;
What the soul itself may cherish
   Never from us fades nor flies.
Hid it may be from the spirit—
   Only for awhile its hid—
And one day will gift our merit
   With a joy to sense forbid.

From our bosom the infernal,
   All that's mean and low and base,
Every wish and longing carnal,
   Chase we then or seek to chase.
Clearer to us then and clearer
   Would Life's complex riddle seem,
And our Edens fled prove nearer
   Than at present we may deem.

Glory-dowered, the task before us
   Then would cease to be a task ;
Then we'd have what could secure us
   Whatsoever we would ask !

Should a thorn then pierce our bosom,
  Even ere the pang had flown,
Even that would turn a blossom
  Our right royal heads to crown.

" Valour's born from self-denial,
  Wisdom from each stern rebuke,
Power from every pain and trial
  That the human soul may brook:"
This or a sublimer burden
  Would express the faith we'd hold,
And a girdle be our guerdon,
  Richer than a girth of gold.

Smiles would leap to hail us victor
  From each flower and running brook;
Beauty would herself impicture
  On whatever we might look.
Stars—the blessed stars, my brother—
  Would attend us in the night,
And Creation's self be other
  Than it seems to common sight.

Up, and gird thee like a warrior!
  Up, and make the present thine;
Trust me, every doubt's a barrier
  To Life's heritage divine!
Sagest heroes, heroic sages
  So have taught since time began.
Up, and earn a heroe's wages!
  Up then—up, and be a man!

BLIGHTED HOPES.

THE hopes that allured me
To cope with the worst,
At length have secured me
The tortures accurst,
Of fever and grief,
And frenzy—in brief
Ills—ills from which Death is the only relief.

But Titan-like lieth
My soul in her chains—
Hourly she sigheth,
The answer she gains,
But adds night and day
To pain and dismay—
'Tis the scream of the vulture despair at his prey.

———

NANNY TO BESSY.

ELEVEN long winters departed
Since you and he sailed o'er the main?
Dear, dear—I've been thrice broken-hearted,
And thrice—but, ah, let me refrain.—

There was not a lassie in Plessy,
    Nay, truly there was not a lad,
That morning you left us all, Bessy,
    But dropped a kind tear and look'd sad.

A week ere ye went ye were married—
    Yes, yes, I remember aright ;
The lads and the lassies all hurried
    To dance at your bridals that night.

With others, were Mary from Horton,
    And Harry from over the fields ;
Your prim cousin Peggy from Chirton,
    And diddler Allen from Shields.

Piper Tom, with his pipes in the corner,
    Did pipe till the red morn a-broke ;
And we danced and we sung in our turn, or
    Gave vent to our glee in a joke.

That seems but last night, tho' eleven
    Black winters have flown since, and yet
Ye're bright as yon star in the heaven,
    Whilst I—but I winnot regret.

Ye're just bright and fresh as a rosy.
    As when ye last left us all, just ;
Whilst I am a poor wither'd posy
    The passer has strampt in the dust.

This was not so always ; no, clearly
    —When lassies—the burnie has shown
The rose on your dimpled cheek nearly
    Out-matched by the rose on my own.

Twinn'd sisters appeared we and canny
　　Together we'd link o'er the wold,
When Bessy's bit secrets to Nanny,
　　And Nanny's to Bessy were told.

Nay's one, we grew up until Harry
　　Was mine—but, was mine for how long?
Then, the changes that followed,—the worry,
　　The guilt, and the shame, and the wrong?

—Ye knew my 'curst bane and besetter?
　　Brown?　Piers with the thievish black e'e?
He danced at your wedding, and better
　　Than any but Harry danced he.

The sight sent the lasses a-skarling,
　　Whenever he came into view;
And many a fond mother's darling
　　Has lived his deception to rue.

Meg Wilson, a-down the green loning,
　　Skipped with him a fine afternoon;
When last she went there she was moaning,
　　Her heart like a harp out of tune.

Even Cary, the dour-looking donnet,
　　Who'd looked on my downfall with scorn,
Was smit with his blink, and her bonnet
　　One Monday was found in the corn.

Nay, many with him tripped and tumbled
　　As I'd tripped and tumbled—what then?
Not one by her fall was so humbled,
　　Or put to one half of my pain.

When Harry was brought on a barrow,
 A corpse from the pit, had I known
—But Brown, who had long been his marrow,
 Then, who was so kind as Piers Brown?

He showed himself ready and willing
 To lighten the load I endured ;
He gather'd me many a shilling,
 And whatso I needed procured.

The bones of my Harry right duly
 Were laid in the grave by his aid ;
Then slipt he to see me—too truly
 So slipt till my pride was low laid.

There's many to point and to titter
 At one who has happen'd a fall—
And into the cup that is bitter,
 The petty still empty their gall.

There's many to point and to titter
 At one that has happen'd to fall—
And into my potion so bitter,
 The petty so emptied their gall.

Then mine was a hardship and trouble,
 When touch'd by deceit's magic mace,
My pride went away like a bubble—
 Then mine was a pitiful case.

Then deep on my cheek burn'd the scarlet,
 The token of sin and of shame ;
And many did call me a harlot,
 More worthy than I of the name.

Then mishap to mishap, like billow
　　To billow succeeded, and I
Was laid with my head on my pillow,
　　And no one to solace me nigh.

Then perished the darlings you kindly
　　Remember and ask for—alorn,
I lay by the morsels and blindly,
　　Then cursed the dark hour I was born.

A-lorn by the dead lay I—driven
　　To frenzy by grief, shame and scorn,
And lifted my two hands to heaven,
　　Then cursed the dark hour I was born.

I cursed—felt accursed—nay, that hourly
　　I'd dogg'd by a black devil been ;
And he, when he'd speeded most surely,
　　Had held in derision my teen.

He'd dazzled and led me to yamour,
　　For baubles one ought to despise,
Then whipt from my vision the glamor,
　　And shown the sad truth to my eyes.

He'd mounted the air, and a snelling
　　Bleak blast had swept valley and plain,
And the dwelling of joy made the dwelling
　　Of dire, desolation and pain.

Years long the keen thought of the cruel
　　Black lot of thy crony a-made
Her thus feel and thus prate, and—ah jewel !—
　　Did put a mill-wheel in her head.

Their cold looks and words a-pierced only
   Skin deep in the end at the most ;
But ah, for the hours dark and lonely
   The thought of the jewels yet cost.

The pale morning finds me a-wringing
   My hands for the dearies in vain ;
The day passes by without bringing
   Me any relief to my pain.

Evermore on my heart feeds the canker,
   The cruel reflection that—ay—
That they for a morsel did hanker,
   I had not a penny to buy.

Overcome by despair in confusion
   Of mind, I will wander oft ; when
The prey of a charming delusion,
   They seem to me living again.

Again on their hazels a-prancing,
   They hie as they hied o'er the way,
The midges above them a-dancing,
   Are not half so merry as they.

Again up and down the ball boundeth,
   A-tween their bit hands and the earth,
Till rapture their senses confoundeth,
   And laughter gives vent to their mirth.

Again—in my sight—my woe banished,—
   The birds seem a-living again,
Then quickly I find them a-vanished,
   And sorrow yet with me, and pain.

While yet but a lassie, I married;
  While yet in my teens I was left;
Ere olden to frenzy was harried—
  Ere olden of hope I'm a-reft.

A reed by the wild wind a-broken
  Am I, and my tongue in vain seeks
To utter the tale which a-spoken,
  Would hurry that rose from your cheeks

But let me refrain.   Since we parted—
  Ah lass, since ye went o'er the main;
Since then I've been thrice broken-hearted,
  And thrice—but ah, let me refrain.

———

GET UP.

"Get up," the caller calls, "Get up!"
    And in the dead of night,
  To win the bairns their bite and sup,
    I rise a weary wight.

  My flannel dudden donn'd, thrice o'er
    My birds are kissed, and then,
  I with a whistle shut the door,
    I may never ope again.

THE LAD OF BEBSIDE.

My heart is away with the lad of Bebside,
And never can I to another be tied ;
Not, not to be titled a lord's wedded bride,
Could Jenny abandon the lad of Bebside.
      My heart is away, &c.

There's many a laddie as brave as can be,
Distracted to win a kind glance from my e'e ;
But all the sweet favours, that I can provide,
Are hoarded with care for the lad of Bebside.
      My heart is away, &c.

He dances so clever, he whistles so fine,
He's flattered and wooed from the "Wans" to the
    " Tyne ;"
Yet a scorner to falsehood, a stranger to pride,
I'm alone the beloved of the lad of Bebside.
      My heart is away, &c.

To our house he repair'd on the eve of last Fair,
And cracked with my mother, my mother so dear ;
Next morning right early with spleen I was eyed
To link to the Fair with the lad of Bebside.
      My heart is away, &c.

Last night at the dancing, 'mid scores of fine queans,
The eldest among them scarce out of her teens,
He chose me, and truly with heart overjoyed,
I footed the jig with the lad of Bebside.
      My heart is away, &c.

To wed me he's promised, and ill fare the tongue
Would whisper such laddie such lassie could wrong ;
The moon's on the wane—ere another be spied,
I'll lie in the arms of the lad of Bebside.

       My heart is away with the lad of Bebside.

MEG GOLDLOCKS.

YE'VE heard of Meg Goldlocks of Willington Dene ?
The stoniest damsel that ever was seen ;
Yet, her beauty distress'd, with its splendour, the rest
Of the lasses for miles around Willington Dene.

       Ye've heard of Meg Goldlocks, &c.

Meek Mary of Howdon, with Robin would rove !
But once to the Dene should his roguish feet move,
A-jealous of Meg's unmatched beauty, her tongue
Was turned to a bell, and a merry peal rung.

       Ye've heard of Meg Goldlocks, &c.

Blythe Betsy of Percy, eyed Jim like a spy,
Lest o'er to the Dene he should slip on the sly ;
Nay, did she but dream it, with heart like to break,
She scowled when she met him for all the next week.

       Ye've heard of Meg Goldlocks, &c.

Sweet Nancy of Benton, deemed Willie her own,
Till he went to the Dene on an errand unknown ;
The errand to her was apparent as day,
And the rose on her dimpled cheek withered away.

       Ye've heard of Meg Goldlocks, &c.

Thus matters went on around Willington Dene,
Till East came a gallant and married the quean ;
That moment the rest of the lasses were blest,
And their lovers allowed to tread Willington Dene !
Ye've heard of Meg Goldlocks, &c.

THE FAIRIES' ADIEU.

"Our revels now are ended, so good night,so good night,
And each unto our chamber let us hie,
And there lose ourselves in visions till the broad daylight
Again has bid adieu unto the sky.
So good bye
Till day has gone out of the sky."

"My couch is in the daisy with its golden, golden eye,"
"And mine is in the violet, sweet and pure,"
"And mine the modest blue bell, beneath whose canopy
I dream away the angry day secure.
"So good bye
Till day has gone out of the sky.

"But when the day's departed, upstarting from our
dreams
We'll gather in a ring upon the green,
And there dance till night's enraptured, and the pale
moon seems
To mourn the fate that changeth such a scene.
So good bye
Till day has gone out of the sky."

THE RING.

THO' many a moon had roll'd away
    ˙ Since Essex at the block had died,
The Queen upon her night-couch lay,
    And o'er his end horrific sighed.

" Oh Essex, oh ! my joy and woe
    Did on thy joy and woe depend ;
And Essex I was doomed to sigh,
    That day which saw thy dismal end.

" The ring I gave in moments fled,
    Had'st thou to me that ring but sent,
Thy precious blood had not been shed,
    These bosom chords had not been rent.

" But thou would'st die, and I must sigh,
    Tho' slander dogs the heels of fame,
And would deny the fact that I
    Could ever feel affection's flame.

" They say I'm proud, tho' not aloud—
    It's spoken in a bitter tone ;
Tho' not aloud, they say I'm proud,
    And that my heart's a heart of stone.

" Ah, could the world the veil up-lift—
    These tinsel trappings—and survey
My soul on storm-tost seas adrift,
    How would they start at the display ?

" My tenderness has not come short
    Of hers whose tears had thawed the churl ;
I've been the dupe, if not the sport,
    Of passions worthy of a girl.

" And he on whom my hope was built,
Ah, even he, a cruel act !—
Immersed me in a sea of guilt,
Then left me with a bosom rack'd.

" How could his pride the block have dyed
With his own crimson drops, before
To me he'd yield, to me his shield,
From faction's fangs in days of yore.

" How could—but was't his pride so vast
Upon himself the blow that dealt ?
In agony what if I sigh
For one who mocked the touch I felt ?

" For one who scorned the royal ire ?
Despised the feelings of this breast ?
Possess'd me with a base desire,
To make of me a brothel jest ?

" Awake my soul ! exert thy power—
Another mine terrific sprung—
Take up thy burden, and this hour
Be, be it into Lethe flung.

" Awake, and—oh ! "—thus did she sigh—
" Thou cruel Essex ! "—when her ears
Are startled by a din, and by
Her side a troubled dame appears.

" The Lady Nottingham to-night—
This hour—upon her death-bed lies,
And lying in this woeful plight
' Go, bring the Monarch ! ' raves and cries.

" A secret rankles in her soul,
The which she seems right fain to speak ;
But when she tries her eye-balls roll,
And heavy sighs the sentence break."

For coach and steed at this with speed.
 The Great Eliza calls, and see !
Soon Queen and guard, and coach and steed,
 Away into the darkness flee.

Away o'er hills and dales they dart,
 A hare-hound from the leash away !
The birds from out the hedges start
 And fly; confounded with dismay.

Echo awakes her myriad tongues,
 And with the tones of wild despair,
The clang of wheel and hoof prolongs ;
 —Harsh music on the midnight air !

Roods, miles are pass'd, and shouts of "Queen !"
 Soon thro' a castle's halls are heard,
Where you may see a wan dame's mien
 Change at the sound of that dread word.

Yet mark not this yon woeful band,
 Who with o'erburden'd feelings watch
That moment when death's clay-cold hand
 Shall life from her endearments snatch.

In truth the tear bedims their sight,
 And had conceal'd the fact, that they
Possessed a light more pure and bright
 Than what their sickly lamps display.

Too, man's but man ; and how-be-it
 The spirit would her task fulfil,
The senses weary and remit
 Their aptness to obey the will.

Three nights have vanished since her end
 Appear'd but on the threshhold ; lo !
A bitter thing to see a friend
 Thus struggling with the common foe.

So feel they, muse they, cry " ah, me ! "
Or whisper low, or shake the head,
When nears the mighty Queen, and see !
The dying riseth on her bed.

The band that binds her hair unties,
Her hair a-down her shoulders strays ;
A gleam re-lights her sunken eyes,
And o'er her ghastly features plays.

" Well thou art here," she gasps, " and well
With death I've striven to reveal
What, what it racks my soul to tell,
And doubly racks it to conceal.   .

" When he who late for treason bled,
Had let the Spanish feel his sword,
The fame on which his spirit fed,
Was it not graced by your regard ?

" Then gave you not to him a ring,
Averring ' If at any time
Thou shalt my frown upon thee bring,
Show that, and I'll forgive the crime ? '

" He took that ring, the period came
When he did need its magic might ;
He gave it me to give—my shame !—
It never met his monarch's sight.

" My lord to Essex being a foe,
Prevailed on me to keep the boon ;
The rest is known."—A moment, lo !
Her majesty is turned to stone.

Her late flushed cheeks are bleak and blanched,
Her eyes shoot forth a frantic glare ;
Her lips are writhed, her hands are clenched,
And in their grasp her up-torn hair.

" Hell and damnation eat thee up—
    The seven vials the prophet saw
Be 't thine " at last she cried, " to sup,
    For this base breach of human law.

" Great God protect me, I am mad—
    This trial is too much for one
With might until this moment clad
    To trample death and terror down.

" Kingdoms have trembled at my frown,
    Or at my smile have danced for joy;
But now the star of glory's flown,
    That shone upon the hours gone by.

" Ah, never more ! ah, never more
    Will joy, will peace to me return ! "
This said, she sank upon the floor,
    And there remained her woes to mourn.

Nor could she be consoled, nor would,
    But rather nursed her mind's distress ;
Till sorrow gave her to her shroud,
    And thus did end the Good Queen Bess.

NOTE.

THE RING (page 92).—There is a tradition that Essex had elicited from Queen Elizabeth a ring as a token of confidence, with the assurance that if ever he should incur her displeasure, or need her assistance, by the production of the said ring she should be pacified, or that assistance given. Afterwards the Earl was impeached for high treason, tried, and condemned, when, to the last, the Queen anxiously awaited the forthcoming of the token which should have secured his pardon. The talisman did not come, and the Earl was executed. Years after, the Queen discovered that the Earl had, by a confidant, sent to her the ring, but that from malicious motives it had not been delivered, whereat she went nearly frantic, and died a few days after of a broken heart.

www.ingramcontent.com/pod-product-compliance
Lightning Source LLC
Chambersburg PA
CBHW060245030726
47493CB00025B/2694